HOW TO SAVE A
DRAGON

Annie Dalton

Illustrated by Carl Pearce

HOW TO SAVE A DRAGON
TAMARIND BOOKS 978 1 84853047 8

Published in Great Britain by Tamarind Books
A division of Random House Children's Books
A Random House Group Company

This edition published 2011

1 3 5 7 9 10 8 6 4 2

The Random House Group Limited supports the Forest Stewardship
Council® (FSC®), the leading international forest certification organiation.
All our titles that are printed on Greenpeace approved FSC® certified paper
carry the FSC® logo. Our paper procurement policy can be found at
www.randomhouse.co.uk/environment

Typeset in Bembo MT Schoolbook 16/20pt
by Falcon Oast Graphic Art Ltd.

Tamarind Books are published by Random House Children's Books
61–63 Uxbridge Road, London W5 5SA

www.**tamarindbooks**.co.uk
www.**kids**at**randomhouse**.co.uk
www.**randomhouse**.co.uk

Addresses for companies within The Random House Group Limited can
be found at: www.randomhouse.co.uk/offices.htm

THE RANDOM HOUSE GROUP Limited Reg. No. 954009

A CIP catalogue record for this book is available from the British Library.

Printed and bound by CPI Group (UK) Ltd, Croydon, CR0 4YY

This book is for Sophie & Izzie
(and for anyone who still believes in magic)
AD

For Cen
CP

How we came to World Nine . . .

Once upon a time I lived with my mum
and my baby sister Ruby on a foggy grey
world called Terra Nova. At night the
hoot of foghorns drowned the swoosh of
starships taking off and landing. Terra
Nova is the intergalactic hub for starship
travel — something Mum did a lot of in
her work with the Cosmic Peace Police.

Then, out of the blue, Mum quit her
job. She said she'd had enough of zooming
around the universe stopping wars; it was
time for a change. She'd found us the
perfect house on a faraway planet called
World Nine.

'From now on, Oscar, I'm going to be a
stay-at-home mum,' Mum told me. 'I'm
going to grow vegetables and bake bread
and we're going to live happily ever after.'
We caught a cab to the starport where
Mum bought three tickets to a world so
small the mapmakers hadn't even given

it a proper name. On our tickets the machine had just printed <u>W9</u>.

Our new home on tiny tropical World Nine turned out to be just as wonderful as Mum had promised. But after we moved in we started running into little problems the estate agent had forgotten to mention: mice, leaky pipes — and the fact that some of our neighbours were wizards.

It was our neighbour, Miss Coralie Creek, who let it slip about the wizards when she came to welcome us to the area. Miss Coralie tried to tell my mum that not all wizards were bad but Mum was so upset she stopped listening.

When I got up next morning, my mum was asleep at the kitchen table. She'd been making a list:

<u>Reasons to stay on W9</u>
NO FOG!!
Sun, sea, garden
Children happy

Reasons to leave W9
MAGIC!!!

I was in love with World Nine already, magic and all, so I was thrilled when Mum said she wasn't taking us back to Terra Nova. At least, not yet.

'We'll stay for a trial period to see how we get on. But I'm not sending you to the local school,' Mum said firmly. 'I'm not having you or Ruby mixed up with magic. I'll teach you at home.'

Just days after Mum found out about the wizards, a starship landed on our lawn. Mum's old bosses at the Cosmic Peace Police had come to beg her to do one last crucial mission.

Mum refused. She said there was no one on World Nine she trusted to take care of us.

I told Mum she had to do the mission. I'd figured out a way to keep me and Ruby safe from evil wizards until she got back: we just had to hold a contest to find a genuinely trustworthy wizard.

Mum wasn't happy about it but she eventually agreed.

A teenage wizard called Ferris Fleet aced the competition, with the help of his magical wheelchair, Wonderwheels. Thanks to Fleet, Mum was able to zoom to the other side of the universe, where she successfully prevented a dangerous cosmic war.

I was relieved when my mum was safely home again, but I was disappointed too. I was going to miss having mad adventures with Ferris Fleet. Life was going to be really tame from now on.

That's what I thought.

I was wrong.

Chapter One

FERRIS FLEET DAY

It was Wednesday, my favourite day of the week. The early morning sun felt hot on my bare arms as I jogged down the veranda steps.

I was on a mission for my mum, but for a moment I stopped to watch a tiny hummingbird hovering over a gigantic scarlet flower. If I listened carefully I could hear the waves hitting the rocks way down in Shipwreck Bay. I gave a contented sigh. It was another perfect day on World Nine.

It was three months now since Mum had brought us to live on this tiny tropical planet and I still couldn't believe the sky could be so blue, or leaves so green. World Nine had such bright colours I sometimes needed to put my sunglasses on for a little rest!

'Oscar?' Mum popped her head out of a window, making me jump. 'You still here?'

'I'm on my way!' I told her.

'Shout as soon as you see him coming up the mountain. I want to time the pancakes just right.'

'Got it!'

Mum disappeared again, then totally confused me by popping out of a completely different window. 'I just need

6

to check my starmails then I'll start the pancake batter!'

'You're not checking your messages *again*?' I was just teasing, but Mum's expression turned frosty.

'I worked for the Cosmic Peace Police for ten years, Oscar. I like to keep in touch.'

'So you're not just checking because you want to know if you won this year's All Galaxies Peace Award?' I asked in an innocent voice.

Mum looked seriously flustered now. 'Oscar, I *keep* telling you. Thousands of people have been nominated. I'm *not* going to win. Now get up into that tree house quick-smart and let me know the minute you see him.'

'Yes, ma'am!' I took off at a run, jumping over flowerpots and anything that stood in my way.

I could hear my baby sister's growly little voice floating up from inside the

house. She was singing a song she'd made up. It went, 'Feet, Feet, hurry up, Feet!'

It's not just me who loves Wednesdays. We all do. That's because Wednesday is Ferris Fleet day. Mum was even making pancakes in Fleet's honour and she doesn't do that for just anyone, let alone a wizard.

My mum had never had to deal with wizards until we'd moved here. They didn't exist on Terra Nova. At my old school, magic was actually like a rude word.

After three months on World Nine, Mum is still not a big fan of wizards in general, but she is a huge fan of Ferris Fleet! She absolutely trusts him to take good care of me and Ruby. When she

8

asked Fleet if he would be her regular Wednesday baby-sitter, she made him promise he would never use magic while he's looking after us and he never ever has.

Fleet reckons it's harder for Mum to adapt to World Nine than for me and Ruby. He said grown-ups, especially scientifically minded grown-ups from non-magical worlds – like my mum – are often freaked out by magic. They think it's too wild and scary to be safe. I told him it's a good thing we built my tree house before the big magic ban! Luckily Mum's never asked us exactly *how* we built it, so we didn't even have to lie!

I still get a thrill each time I see my tree house. This morning it was occupied by a family of tiny green parrots. They flew off squawking as I scrambled up to my lookout platform. Fleet and I built it so you can see all the way to the bottom of the mountain.

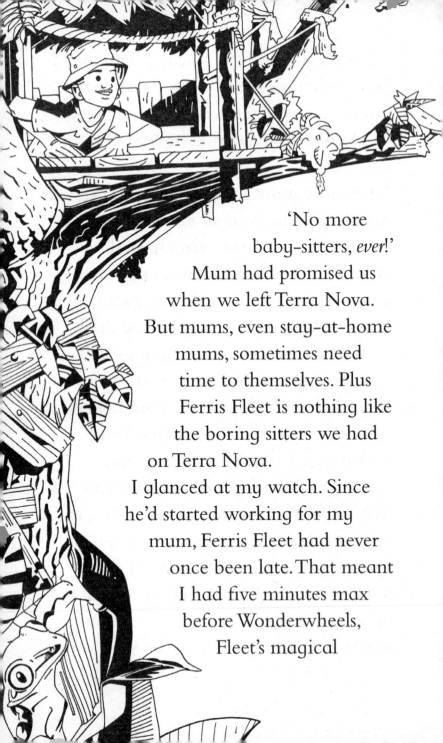

'No more
baby-sitters, *ever*!'
Mum had promised us
when we left Terra Nova.
But mums, even stay-at-home
mums, sometimes need
time to themselves. Plus
Ferris Fleet is nothing like
the boring sitters we had
on Terra Nova.
I glanced at my watch. Since
he'd started working for my
mum, Ferris Fleet had never
once been late. That meant
I had five minutes max
before Wonderwheels,
Fleet's magical

wheelchair, came humming into view.

I settled down to wait. One by one the parrots came back to perch on the branches. I'd never seen a real bird until we moved here. They didn't have birds on Terra Nova. The fog is too toxic. But when you've lived somewhere since you were two years old, a grey, foggy world without birds or magic seems normal.

Perched high in my tree house, I was far away in my thoughts. I almost didn't notice the clear sweet humming sound floating up the mountain. Suddenly I saw bright colours flicker and flash as Wonderwheels flew round the bend. I scrambled back down the ladder and shouted at the top of my voice, 'PUT THE PANCAKES ON, MUM! FERRIS FLEET IS HERE!'

Chapter Two

WOO-HOO, VIPS!

I raced down the track, sending tiny stones
flying. Seconds later, Fleet's wheelchair
zoomed into the front garden, filling the air
with magical hummingbird colours.

With or without magic, Fleet is more
fun than anyone I know. He's funny
and incredibly brave. He's like the big

brother I always wished I had.

When Fleet saw me hurtling towards him, his eyes lit up. 'Hey, Oscar! What's for breakfast this morning?' He had his usual broad smile, but this morning there were faint shadows under his eyes.

I wagged my finger. 'You've been up all night partying!'

He shook his head, laughing. 'Not partying.'

'Studying, then?' Fleet is a student at the wizard university in Lonelyheart, our nearest town.

He swallowed a yawn. 'Not studying, either. I started this wildlife protection thing. It's just a small group of us students. We spent last night camping out in Firebreath Valley. Didn't get much sleep.'

'Oh, right,' I said, disappointed. Fleet had never struck me as the bird-watching type. 'Mum's making her special pancakes. If you like them hot we'd better scoot.'

Ruby was waiting for us on the veranda. When she saw Fleet she shrieked and clapped her hands. Fleet steered his wheelchair smoothly up the veranda steps, scooped up my giggling little sister and we all went inside.

I was expecting Mum to be standing by the stove tossing pancakes like a juggler. I was wrong. There wasn't even a smell of pancakes and Mum was nowhere to be seen. I could hear her voice coming from her office.

'I'd better go and see what's going

on,' I told Fleet.

When Mum saw me she quickly put her hand over the phone. 'I'll just be two ticks!'

After her call ended, she stood staring out of the window without saying a word.

'Mum?'

'I won,' she whispered. She gave me a huge bear hug. 'Woo-whee!! I actually won the award!'

'That's brilliant, Mum!' I gasped when I caught my breath. 'Let's tell Fleet.'

Mum cooked everyone a massive breakfast to celebrate. Fleet and I

toasted her with pineapple and mango smoothies, and Ruby shouted, 'Hip ray!' even though she had *no* clue what was going on.

'What's your award for?' Fleet asked Mum through a mouthful of hot pancake.

'You should know,' I told him. 'You helped her win it! She stopped a war on that seriously creepy planet with three moons.'

Fleet looked amazed. 'I didn't realize it was *that* mission!'

'You should give Ferris Fleet a mention in your acceptance speech,' I teased Mum. 'If we hadn't found Fleet, you never could have gone on that mission. I should get a mention too,' I added with a grin. 'It was me who thought of holding a competition to find a good wizard to protect us while you were away!'

'Yeah? So who won?' Fleet teased.

'*You did*, you silly moose!' I beamed at him. I noticed Mum scribbling one of her to-do lists.

'I'd better book our flights,' she said.

I felt a flicker of panic. 'Why? Where are we going?'

'To Terra Nova, obviously! I've got to collect my award.'

I put down my fork and gulped. 'We don't have to come, do we?'

Mum looked startled. 'Oscar! It's only one of the most important days of my life. Of course I want you and Ruby with me!'

Suddenly I didn't feel like finishing my pancakes. When no one was looking I slipped out to the veranda. After a while Fleet came to find me.

'What's wrong?' he asked quietly.

'I can't go back,' I said.

I told Fleet about my old school
where they made the kids dress in
stupid uniforms like starship troopers
and we were only allowed to read fact
books about space and machines. I told
him about lying in bed listening to the
sad hooting of foghorns and how the
sound always leaked into my dreams.

'I didn't know I hated Terra Nova
before we came here, but I did. I always
hated everything about it.'

Fleet held up his hand. 'Oscar, relax! You're not going back there to *live*. You're going to support your mum. You'll be back home in no time, telling me all about it.'

'Yeah, but—'

Fleet looked stern. 'This is your mum we're talking about. She's got to walk up on stage in front of a hall full of zillions of people. She's going to need you cheering her on.'

'I suppose,' I said reluctantly.

'You never know, this trip might even turn into an adventure!' Fleet clapped me on the back. 'Now, let's go to the beach.'

'Sure you're not too tired from your *wildlife patrol?*' I put on my silly voice.

'No chance! After your mum's

19

pancakes I'm totally turbocharged!'
When we got back a couple
of hours later, Mum had
received some more
exciting news. 'My
old bosses are
paying for us to
fly in one of their
private starships!'
'You're *kidding*!' I
breathed. Only Very
Important People
–VIPs for short
– get to fly in
those. Next
minute, Mum
and I were
jumping around
the kitchen
singing, 'Woo-
hoo, VIPs!
Woo-hoo,
VIPs!'

★

Suddenly everything started happening super-fast. Just two weeks after my mum had got the phone call, we were taking our seats on our VIP starship.

When we'd moved to World Nine, Mum had got us super-cheap tickets. They'd been cheap for a good reason. That space trip took *for ever.* We had to change starships *five* times. This time, the Peace Police starship took us directly to Terra Nova in less than half the time!

I didn't tell Mum, but I was secretly dreading the moment I had to set foot on Terra Nova. When I saw the lights of the starport glowing through the fog I wanted to scream to the pilot, 'TURN BACK NOW!' Then I remembered Fleet saying that I wasn't coming back here to live, and I was able to get a grip.
On our first morning in Terra Nova, Mum took us shopping in one of the huge shopping centres. She bought

a smart suit for me, a cute dress for Ruby, and a seriously swanky frock for herself. I couldn't remember ever seeing my mum in a dress. Usually she wears combats and T-shirts.

The awards ceremony was held that same night. Mum, Ruby and I had to walk down an endless red carpet into a terrifyingly vast hall sparkling with chandeliers.

The ceremony went on for hours and hours. When it was Mum's turn to receive her award, I had to wake Ruby up to clap.

Mum looked totally calm as she made her acceptance speech with

photographers' flashbulbs going off all around. Guess what? She took my advice and thanked Ferris Fleet for making it possible for her to go on the mission in the first place. She said, 'Every time I went on a mission I was trying to make the universe a safer place, not just for my children, Oscar and Ruby, but for children everywhere.' I could have burst with pride!

After the ceremony there was a massive banquet. I really lucked out. I'd been put next to Lily Chilada. I knew Lily because our mums used to work together, plus she was the only one I really clicked with at school.

Lily caused a major ruckus one time. We'd been told to write an essay about life forms that live in the ocean. Lily wrote about mermaids. Mr. Starkweather tore up her essay in front of the class. He made her write out one hundred lines in her best handwriting: *Mermaids don't exist.*

But what Lily actually wrote out 100 times was:

Mermaids don't exist – <u>in this world.</u>

While the grown-ups at the banquet made boring speeches, I told Lily about Mum accidentally buying a house on one of the few surviving magical worlds. Lily's eyes grew huge. Next minute she was scribbling her starmail address on a napkin. 'If you ever see a mermaid you've got to message me straight away!'

'I'll send pics!' I promised.

I was just starting to enjoy the evening when suddenly it was over. We had to go straight to the starport in our fancy award ceremony clothes. In the taxi, Mum

stared around at the huge high-rises looming through the fog. She seemed dismayed. 'I can't believe we ever lived in such an unhealthy place. Did you see how pale Lily was?'

I'd been worrying that going back to Terra Nova would unsettle Mum all over again. I was scared she'd decide that she missed her exciting job with the Cosmic Peace Police and we'd have to live on foggy Terra Nova for ever.

But it was exactly the opposite: Mum said she couldn't wait to go home to our peaceful life in the country!

'Even *with* the wizards?' I asked daringly.

Mum pulled a face. 'Yes, Oscar, even with the wizards. I mean, it's not like I actually have to *marry* one!'

We both laughed at the far-fetched idea of my scientifically minded mum marrying a wizard and, as always, Ruby laughed because we were laughing.

A few minutes later we were on board

the starship, ready to enjoy our last twenty-four hours as Very Important People. We watched all the latest Terra Novan films, working our way through a selection of luxury snacks. Finally I fell asleep.

It seemed like only minutes later that Mum was shaking me awake. 'Oscar, we're coming in to land.'

'How come?' I mumbled, rubbing my eyes. I couldn't tell if it was night or morning – the cabin crew had pulled down the blinds. But I was pretty sure World Nine was still hours away.

'There's some kind of crisis. The CPP need their starship back. We're being diverted to a planet called Zapaduti. Apparently we can get a space bus home from here.'

'Is that an actual *world*?'

'I changed starships there once years ago,' Mum told me. 'It's way out in the cosmic backwaters. Don't be surprised if we run into some really dodgy characters.'

'How dodgy?' I was wide awake and interested now.

'Smugglers, pirates, thieves,' she said casually.

We landed in the middle of the night. It was freezing cold. One of the startroopers gave us a blanket to wrap around my little sister.

The starport on Zapaduti was basically a rusty old shed. There was a handful of other passengers waiting to go to World Nine. *They don't look that dodgy*, I thought, disappointed.

Then I thought, *Except him.*

Chapter Three

NO STAR TOO FAR

A sinister-looking figure was slouched against a broken vending machine. His hands were pushed into the pockets of his long super-size coat and he was whistling the same tune over and over. It was the kind of tune that instantly gets stuck in your brain, but in a creepy way.

He looked at us shivering in our evening clothes and grinned at Mum like a wolf in a cartoon. 'You're a brave young woman bringing two little kids to a place like this,' he sneered.

I gave him my meanest stare. 'We're going home, that's why. And for your

29

information, I'm not a little kid.'

I thought Mum would tell me off. She doesn't approve of kids talking back to adults. Luckily, at that moment, an ancient starbus came thundering in to land. I could see dents where it had been hit by flying space debris. On the side in fading letters, it said: *McCool's Sky Shuttle – No Star Too Far*.

The pilot jumped out and started unloading baskets and crates. Something about him seemed familiar, but I couldn't think what. 'Going to World Nine again?' he said to the man in the coat. 'People will think you've found yourself a girlfriend!' 'I can go where I like so long as I pay my fare,' the traveller growled. He pushed past us onto the starbus, giving us a close-up view of his coat.

From a distance it looked like normal leather, but now I noticed gleams of colour – like those oily rainbows you sometimes get in puddles. A weird scent wafted from him, like smoke or incense. It was so strong and sweet that I felt dizzy.

'I'd feel better if you and your family sat up front with me,' the pilot told Mum.

I'd never sat at the controls of a spaceship before!

We strapped ourselves into our seats and Mum introduced us all to the pilot.

He gave her a lopsided grin. 'Merlin McCool at your service.'

Mum sneaked a glance at the man with the leather coat. He had rolled his coat up for a pillow and seemed to be settling down to sleep. 'Who is that guy?' she asked in a low voice.

'Goes by the name of Windigo,' said McCool. 'No one knows his real name.'

'Is he some kind of crook?'

McCool frowned. 'More like a poacher or hunter. I just wish someone could catch him at it. World Nine has lost too much wildlife already.'

'Did World Nine used to have more wildlife?' Mum asked.

'Once upon a time, World Nine was a home to creatures you couldn't find anywhere else in the universe,' he told her.

Mum laughed. 'You make it sound like a fairy tale.'

'That's exactly what it was like.' McCool sounded perfectly serious. 'Then lowlifes like Windigo started turning up. But let's not talk about them.' He turned to give me his strangely familiar grin. 'Ever flown a ship before, Oscar?'

I shook my head. I knew he was teasing.

'I guess today's the day then,' he said calmly.

Mum said, 'I really don't think—'

'Hey, this is the wild space frontier! We make our own rules! Besides, this old lady knows the way better than me. Relax! It's on autopilot,' he whispered to my mum.

McCool and I swapped seats, then he showed me what to do.

'Remember to breathe and you'll be OK,' he joked.

I soon noticed something peculiar. On the outside, McCool's starbus looked like a real rust-bucket, but once we actually took off she flew as smoothly as the swanky VIP starship we'd left behind.

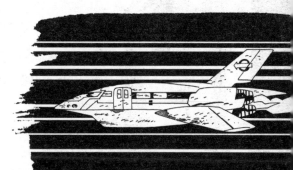

'Can I ask what you guys were doing all the way out in the cosmic boonies?' McCool asked. 'Zapaduti isn't exactly the centre of the Universe!'

'My mum had to go to Terra Nova to collect an award,' I told him proudly before Mum could answer. 'She got it for stopping a war.'

He gave a low whistle. 'Did she? And now I have the honour of flying you back to World Nine. So whereabouts are you celebs living?'

Mum laughed. 'I bought a house between the mountains and the bay.'

'Just outside Lonelyheart, right?' said McCool.

Mum was surprised. 'How did you know?'

McCool grinned his lopsided grin. 'I

34

grew up a few miles down the road. Do you know Miss Coralie?'

'She's our nearest neighbour,' said Mum.

'Next time you see her, tell her that Merlin McCool plans to come back one day for some more of her rose-apple pie.'

I was secretly wishing Mum would take a picture of me flying McCool's ship but they were too busy chatting. McCool wanted to know what had made Mum move to a quiet little planet like World Nine. Mum said she'd wanted us to have a home with a garden like her

great-granny had back on Earth.

'World Nine is the right place to start a garden,' McCool told her. 'If you plant a stick before breakfast it'll be sending out shoots by night!'

'It's a beautiful little world,' Mum agreed. 'I'm glad I've decided to stay.'

'Why, were you going to leave?' he asked.

She took a deep breath. 'When I bought the house, I didn't know about the wizards.'

'I'm guessing you're not too keen on them,' McCool said.

'I'm not keen on magic full stop,' Mum said. 'It scares me actually.'

McCool gave her a sideways look. 'That's a shame, because magic is what World Nine does best.'

Before Mum could answer I interrupted. 'Isn't that World Nine over there?'

McCool looked surprised we'd got

there so soon. He said he'd never known time go by so fast.

We quickly swapped seats again.

'Hold onto your hats, folks.' McCool chuckled. 'We're going down.' And like a swirly green marble, World Nine came spinning up to meet us.

After we'd landed, McCool helped Mum with our luggage. 'I might swing by for a visit some time,' he told her. 'See how your garden is coming on.'

I caught Mum smiling to herself as we walked away. When she saw me looking, she quickly changed her expression.

'Were you grinning just then?' I asked.

She gave me a frosty look. 'Certainly not.'

'You so were.' I smirked.

My little sister must have got overtired. She suddenly threw herself on the dirty

floor of the starport and started kicking
and screaming. Mum was busy calming
her down, so she didn't see Windigo
come up behind me.

'So what about you, little boy?' he
hissed in my ear. 'Are you scared of
magic like your mum?'

'No,' I told him fiercely.

'You should be,' he said.

I wanted to move away from him, but
it was like that bad dream where your

legs feel totally rooted to the spot. Then Mum called my name really sharply. The familiar sound of her voice broke the spell and I shakily ran back to join her.

'What was that creep saying to you?' Mum asked.

I shrugged. 'Nothing.' I didn't want to admit how much he'd scared me.

We walked out of the starport into tropical sunshine. I waited with our luggage while Mum went to find a taxi. Somewhere nearby I could hear someone whistling a familiar creepy tune, but I didn't turn round. I already knew it was Windigo . . .

Chapter Four

THE THREE BETTYS

The next day I woke up super-early. I went out onto the veranda and found Mum watching the sun rise over the mountain and sipping her morning coffee with a thoughtful expression. Beside her on our battered old garden table was her latest to-do list. I took a quick peek.

Dig new bed for sweet potatoes
Get Miss Coralie's recipe for
    rose-apple jam
Buy wool and knitting pattern

That's the thing about my mum. Once

she makes up her mind to do something – stop a war on a strange planet, plant a garden, be a stay-at-home mum – she does it one hundred per cent.

For the next few days, Mum was like one of those mothers in a TV advert: baking bread and delicious cakes, picking rose-apples along the mountain track, then turning them into jam. It had taken a while, but Mum was finally settling into life on World Nine.

One afternoon we were drinking iced tea on the veranda when Miss Coralie stopped by.

Mum had just baked a cake, so she invited Miss Coralie to stay for tea. We showed our neighbour the photos I'd taken at the awards ceremony. Miss Coralie started chatting about her useless teenage nephew, Raymond. He'd come to help paint her house and had ended up eating all the food in her fridge. Now he'd disappeared again, leaving her with one half of her house painted kingfisher blue and the other half a peeling, shabby green.

'I just remembered,' Mum said. 'We met an old friend of yours, Merlin McCool. He asked us to give you a message. He said he'll be back for some more of your rose-apple pie one of these days.'

Miss Coralie laughed so hard she cried. 'Oh, my!' she gasped. She took out a hanky and dried her eyes. 'That rascal! When he was a little boy he stole a freshly baked rose-apple pie I'd left out to cool. That's what he meant about coming back for more.'

Mum pretended to be shocked. 'To think I was carrying messages for a thief!'

Miss Coralie shook her head, still chuckling. 'Merlin McCool was always full of mischief. But there was never any harm in him.'

A mockingbird landed on the rail of our veranda and burst into song. Mum watched it with a dreamy expression as the old lady chatted away.

Miss Coralie said she loved all the improvements Mum had made. 'A house needs a woman's touch,' she told Mum. 'I don't think you ever met old Mr Biffin who lived here before?'

Mum shook her head. 'The first time I saw this house

was the day we moved in! It sounds crazy to buy a house I'd never seen, but the minute I saw it online it seemed so right.' Mum was still watching the bird. 'Did you know Mr Biffin very well?' she asked.

The old lady suddenly looked flustered. 'I didn't exactly know him. I heard that he did a lot for charity though.'

Mum nodded. 'I knew he had to be a lovely man. This house has such a special vibe. I felt it the moment we walked in.'

Miss Coralie patted her hand. 'I think you're very brave, dear, coming to a strange world, living here all alone.'

'She's not alone. She's got us,' I said. 'Our mum used to work for the Cosmic Peace Police. She isn't scared of anything. OK, maybe spiders.'

Miss Coralie nodded and smiled. 'Oh, I see. So you probably came across them all the time in your work?'

Mum looked confused. 'Spiders?'

Miss Coralie chuckled. 'No, wizards, silly!'

This misunderstanding sent everyone into fits of the giggles, including Mum. I remembered when she first found out about the wizards – she'd gone flying around our house in a mad panic, locking doors and windows, trying to make it wizard-proof. She was way more relaxed these days. Maybe one day she'd actually let me go to the local school with the other World Nine kids. I really hoped so, but I wasn't holding my breath.

The morning after Miss Coralie's visit, Mum asked if I'd help her in the garden. 'I want to plant sweet potatoes, but I keep finding all this rubbish.'

Mum and I slaved for hours. By lunch time we'd uncovered a mountain of old

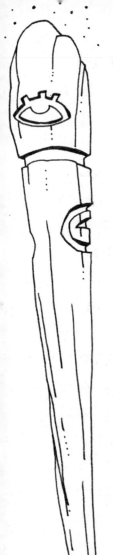

pots, pans, bottles and broken china. Our best find was an old henhouse.

Mum was thrilled. 'I always wanted to keep hens. A few nails and it'll be good as new.'

Before we could move it, we had to unwind miles of flowering creeper. Underneath we found more pots and a broken chair.

'Mr Biffin's relatives must have dumped it when they cleared out his house,' said Mum. 'They even threw away his old walking stick, look.' She dragged something out of the weeds and waved it at me.

When I saw the weird patterns carved on Mr Biffin's stick, I had to stop myself from ducking. Mum hadn't found a walking stick. She'd found a wizard's staff!

'Why don't I put it in the stand with the umbrellas?' I suggested hastily. 'We can use it for knocking down rose-apples next year.' My heart was beating so hard it was a wonder that Mum didn't hear. I gingerly took the stick from her and raced back with it to the house.

'Can you bring me a hammer and nails when you come back?' I heard Mum call.

I carefully propped the staff beside the brollies which Mum insisted we'd need just as soon as the rainy season began, then quickly backed away, rubbing my palms on my jeans. I could feel a strange tingling where I'd touched the staff.

I looked out of the window at Mum cheerfully flinging more rubbish on the pile. *Please don't let her find a spell book*, I thought.

Mum was finally relaxing into her new life on a magical world. She wouldn't feel so relaxed if she found out that this sweet old house had once belonged to a wizard!

With a rush of relief I remembered that tomorrow was Wednesday – Ferris Fleet day. *Fleet will know what to do*, I thought gratefully. I ran to find the hammer and nails.

Once the henhouse was properly fixed, I helped to scrub it clean. Then Mum called a man she found in the phone book and asked if he'd sell us three hens. To our delight, he said he'd bring them right away.

When Ruby saw the hens she actually fell over laughing!

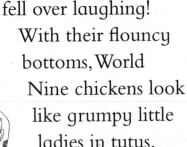

With their flouncy bottoms, World Nine chickens look like grumpy little ladies in tutus.

'What shall we call the birdies?' Mum asked my little sister.

'Betty!' Ruby said at once. Ruby had a rag doll called Betty.

'What, all of them?' I said.

'Can you tell them apart, Oscar?' Mum asked, laughing. 'They look identical to me!'

They looked identical to me too, so we just called them 'the Three Bettys'. We scattered chicken food, filled their trough with clean water, and left them to explore their new home.

Mum and I were both chuffed with our day's work. We walked back to the house swinging my little sister between us. When we reached the veranda Mum suddenly looked annoyed.

'Oscar, what were you thinking, leaving that old stick on the veranda where anyone could trip over it? You said you'd put it with the umbrellas.'

I stared at the wizard's staff in dismay. 'I thought I did,' I said truthfully. 'Sorry, Mum. I'll do it now.'

For the second time I propped Mr Biffin's staff beside the brollies. This time the magic tingle in my palms was so strong it actually made me giggle.

'Cut it out!' I told it sternly. 'Could you please try to look just a bit more like a normal walking stick?'

I blinked and rubbed my eyes. For a moment I thought I'd seen tiny purple sparks. I peered more closely at the staff.

For some reason it didn't look quite

so magic now. It looked like – well, a
walking stick.

'No way, Oscar,' I told myself shakily.
'No way did you just do magic.'

And I ran off to see what Mum was
cooking for tea.

Chapter Five

THE DRAGON-SKIN COAT

By the next day, it was so hot all I
wanted to do was to lie in the shade and
pant like a dog while I waited for Ferris
Fleet to arrive.

No chance.

Can you believe Mum had come up
with a special Wednesday to-do list? She
said what with the house and garden
and flying about the universe collecting
awards, she had let my lessons slide. Now
she wanted Fleet to help her put this right.

This was the item at the top of her list:

Help Oscar with his maths and
spelling

This was the second item:

Take Ruby and Oscar to the library

After a boring hour doing sums and spelling – Mum actually stayed with us so she could see how I was getting on – it was time for Item Two on her list.

Going to the library meant jogging along baking hot country lanes beside Fleet and Ruby in Wonderwheels. At least Fleet and I finally had the chance to talk.

As soon as we were on our own, I told Fleet about Mr Biffin's staff and how it had magically moved from the umbrella stand to the veranda. 'I asked it to stop looking so magic. I never thought it was listening! Next minute there were all these little purple sparks flying about! Now it just looks like an old walking stick again.'

Fleet looked thoughtful. 'It sounds as if you woke it up. The best thing is not to look at it or even think about it. Then the magic will probably go back to sleep.'

I gulped. 'What if I think about it by mistake?'

He laughed. 'Don't worry so much. Using magic is like training a puppy. You have to show it who's boss.'

After the sweltering heat outside, the town library felt blissfully cool. It actually looked more like a shabby old palace than a library. It had more books than Terra Novan libraries but fewer computers.

Fleet read a baby book to Ruby while I investigated the children's section. I

took down a
book with a
battered cover
that looked as
if it had been
borrowed a zillion times, and opened it
at random. The library was suddenly full
of silvery moonlight. I heard the rustle of
leaves and the faraway hoot of an owl.
'Good morning, Oscar,' said a deep voice.

I slammed the book shut. 'Fleet!' I
hissed.

He came whizzing up in his
wheelchair to see what was wrong. I
pointed to the book with a shaking
finger. 'Something spoke. It knew my
name!'

'You're in the *Live Books* section,'
Fleet explained. 'Your mum wouldn't
want you to borrow those. Try the
shelves over there.' He laughed at my
spooked expression. 'Don't worry, those
won't talk.'

I followed Fleet as he did a smart U-turn in Wonderwheels and went humming over to a different section. 'Try these,' he suggested.

'They don't let school kids in Terra Nova read made-up stuff like this.' I held up a book about dragons.

Fleet shook his head. 'Dragons aren't made up. There used to be hundreds on World Nine.'

My mouth dropped open. 'Seriously? They're not just in stories?'

'No, they're not just in stories.' For some reason Fleet looked upset.

'You said there used to be hundreds of dragons on World Nine,' I said. 'Aren't there any more?'

Fleet's voice was suddenly husky. 'No, not any more. Finish choosing your books and we'll go and get a cold drink.'

I borrowed a ton of books, including the dragon one. Then we went to a pavement café and found a table in the shade.

'Tell me about the dragons,' I begged.

'I'm not sure where to start,' said Fleet. 'There were so many kinds. Dragons tiny enough to ride on your shoulder, giant dragons bigger than the biggest starship. Air dragons, water dragons, fire dragons . . .'

I tried to imagine looking up to see a dragon the size of a starship flying over the town.

Something bad must have

happened to these magical creatures or Fleet wouldn't look so sad.

'Aren't there any dragons left at all?' I asked anxiously.

Fleet noticed Ruby about to pour her drink over her head and grabbed her cup. 'Maybe thirty fire dragons have survived. Most of those are pretty old and creaky by now.'

'What happened to the others?'

'People saw a way to make money.'

'What do you mean?'

'They came to this beautiful little world. They saw oceans where mermaids played, secret forests where phoenixes built their nests, and they heard cash registers go *ker-ching*!!'

Ruby was struggling to get down. Fleet quickly gave her his keys to jingle.

'You're telling me that World Nine had dragons and mermaids and phoenixes?' I said.

Fleet nodded.

I remembered Merlin McCool telling Mum that World Nine had once been home to creatures you couldn't find anywhere else in the universe. I'd never dreamed he'd meant *magical* creatures.

'I don't get how the lowlifes make money out of the dragons and phoenixes, though,' I said, frowning. 'Someone's got to notice if you smuggle a dragon onto a starship!'

'True, but it's easy enough to smuggle a dragon skin or an egg,' said Fleet.

I gulped. 'They've been stealing dragons' *eggs?*'

Fleet nodded.

'Can they hatch if they're taken from their mums?'

'Unlikely,' said Fleet grimly.

'So what's the point of taking them?' I heard my voice shake.

'If something's rare enough, people want to own it for themselves, and other people are happy to sell it to them for lots of money.'

'And they don't care that one day there'll be no more eggs and no more dragons?' I felt sick.

Fleet shook his head. 'No. They don't care.'

Ruby was bored with the keys. She started to cry. A waiter hurried over. Picking up a paper napkin, he deftly fashioned it into a

miniature bunny rabbit, then calmly
went back to waiting at tables, leaving
the tiny creature to hop about among
the cake crumbs.

None of the other customers
even blinked.

Ruby was enchanted.
'Little tiny!' she said,
beaming. 'I stroke
it!' She stroked the
magic rabbit gently
with a finger.

Fleet pulled a face.
'Oops. I promised your mum we
wouldn't use magic.'

'*We* didn't,' I pointed out.

I went back to looking at the fire-
breathing dragon on the cover of my
library book. 'How could you take an
egg from that?' I asked in awe. 'She'd
frizzle you like a bacon rasher.'

Fleet lowered his voice to a whisper.
'Of all the hunters, dragon-chasers are

the most patient and cunning. They study dragons for years to learn their habits. For instance, did you know that dragons sing to each other?'

I laughed in amazement.

'It's more like whistling than singing,' said Fleet. 'It sounds quite eerie when several of them are singing together.'

'Whistle a dragon tune now,' I begged.

Fleet shook his head. 'Dragon music is strictly for dragons – it's not meant for people to use. Especially not wizards. Dragon songs can get inside your head and change you. Not in a good way,' he added.

'Are dragon-chasers wizards then?' I asked.

'Most of them,' Fleet said grimly. 'You'd better hope you never run into one and find out.'

I'd stopped listening. I was imagining the starmail I would write to Lily Chilada:

Dear Lily,
Tell Mr Starkweather that World Nine
has real dragons. They sing to each
other like birds.
Best wishes, Oscar.
PS Plus, tell him mermaids <u>do</u> exist,
so nur!

Fleet took a deep breath. 'Oscar, can you keep a secret? That student wildlife group I belong to. It's for protecting dragons.'

I gasped. 'You're kidding!'

'We regularly hike down to Firebreath Valley where a few surviving dragons still live. We want the dragon-chasers to know we're on to them.' Fleet dropped his voice. 'A couple of nights ago we found an egg that had rolled into a gully.'

I thought my heart was going to jump out of my chest. 'You found a real live dragon's egg?'

'We move it to a different hiding place every day. We're worried a dragon-chaser might have followed us back to town.'

'Shouldn't you just take the egg back to its mum?' I objected. 'You said they don't hatch if they're taken away.'

Fleet looked away. 'We went to look for her. She was dead.'

'Oh.' I stared down at the dragon on my book cover. I had a new hopeful thought. 'Couldn't you find another female dragon to help hatch out the egg? Like a foster-mother, kind of?'

He shook his head. 'We think the dead dragon might have been the last breeding female dragon in Firebreath Valley. The other females are too old to lay eggs, and the dragon-chasers have made them scared and

jumpy. This could be the last dragon's egg that was ever laid on World Nine. It probably won't hatch, but we've got to give it a fighting chance.'

Fleet went to pay for our drinks while I waited with Ruby.

When we first arrived on World Nine, I'd been like a tourist, always wondering who the wizards were and who were ordinary World Niners. Now I didn't care. Wizards or no wizards, this world was where I belonged. *I want to be like Fleet*, I thought. *I want to save dragons.*

My sister started to toddle after a passing dog. 'No you don't, missy!' I grabbed her just in time, as someone went barging past; some moron heading for the Merry Oyster Inn, a famously dodgy wizard's hang-out on the other side of the street. 'Hey, watch where you're going!' I shouted.

But he'd already vanished

through the door.

I didn't get a proper
look at him, but I felt
a flicker of fear. I had
caught the faintest whiff of smoke. For a
moment I was back at the starport, with
Windigo's chilling whisper in my ear. I
remembered his coat of strange rainbow-
coloured leather. I remembered how my
legs had totally refused to move.

You're imagining things, I told myself
quickly. *Windigo must have left World Nine
ages ago.*

Fleet came humming towards us. 'Get
ready to roll, Oscar! We're running late!'

That evening Mum and I sat on the
veranda. Fireflies danced around us like
fizzing sparks.

Mum was knitting a sweater for Ruby.

I was reading up on dragons. The book
said dragons have brilliant eyesight for
seeing over distances – flying high over

the rain forest, for instance – but when
they have to look at something close up
they're almost blind. They rely on their
sense of smell to ward off danger.

The book said that when a dragon
died, all its magic went into its skin,
turning it all the colours of a rainbow.

It was a warm night but I went cold
inside. Now I knew why Windigo's
leather coat looked so magical, and why
it smelled of smoke.

It was made of dragon skin.

Chapter Six

WINDIGO THE DRAGON-CHASER

'You're being unusually quiet, Oscar,'
Mum said at breakfast.

'I feel unusually quiet,' I told her.

And stupid, I thought. I'd been mentally
kicking myself all night. I kept hearing
that creepy tune Windigo was whistling
on Zapaduti. I knew what he'd been
whistling now. It was a dragon song.

Dragon-chasers are the most patient
and cunning of all the hunters, Fleet
had said. Windigo was cunning all right.
Teaching himself to whistle the secret
songs dragons used to talk to each
other, wearing a dragon-skin coat that
reeked of dragon smoke. A short-sighted

dragon could be temporarily tricked into believing Windigo was a dragon too – until it was too late.

Now that World Nine's dragons were dying out, Windigo was having to be more cunning than ever, skulking around on World Nine until he finally had something to take back to his wealthy buyers.

Deep down I had known it was Windigo I'd seen at the Merry Oyster. I just hadn't wanted to believe it. Now I was desperate to warn Fleet.

I'd tried phoning his lodgings, but Mrs Strange – his landlady – said he'd gone out first thing.

'Oscar? Are you sure you're OK?' Mum was looking genuinely worried now.

'I'm fine,' I fibbed. 'Just a bit tired.'

'Are you up to looking after Ruby for a while?' she asked. 'I want to make some bread.'

I attempted a smile. 'Sure, no probs.'

Anything was better than torturing myself with 'what ifs'. What if Windigo had overheard our conversation? What if he'd followed Fleet and his friends to Firebreath Valley and forced them to show him where they were hiding the egg?

While Mum mixed a batch of bread dough I took Ruby to sit on the swing seat old Mr Biffin had left behind on the veranda. My little sister called anything with wings 'birdie', even beetles and bats! So I started teaching her the proper names of the birds she could see flying around our garden: parrots, mockingbirds, hummingbirds and kiskadees.

Mum came out with flour on her hands. 'Phone!' she shouted.

It was Fleet.

'Where've you been, man?' I complained. 'I left a million messages!'

'I've been revising for my end- of-year wizarding exams,' Fleet said. 'What's up? You sound upset.'

I told him about Windigo, that I was almost sure I'd seen him in town.

'You seriously think he's our dragon-chaser?' Fleet sounded as if he wasn't sure whether to believe me.

'Our starbus pilot said Windigo was dodgy. He said he's always coming back to World Nine. McCool reckons he's a hunter or a poacher.'

'McCool?' Fleet's voice changed. 'You met Merlin McCool?'

'Yes, do you know him?'

'I know him very well,' said Fleet. 'If he thinks Windigo is dodgy, he probably is.'

'Windigo always smells of smoke,' I said. 'Not normal smoke. It made me go dizzy. And he wears this big coat that comes right down over the tops of his boots.' I swallowed hard. 'Fleet, I think it's made of dragon skin. It's tough like leather, but there are mixed-up colours glinting in it.'

There was a short pause, then I heard Fleet say huskily, 'Yeah, that's dragon skin.'

'Tell the police, Fleet. Tell them he's walking around in a dragon-skin coat!

How much proof do they need?!'

'Oscar, calm down. I can't tell the police.'

'Why not?'

'World Nine doesn't have a police force. Magical worlds handle things differently.'

I felt like tearing my hair out. 'So how do we stop Windigo getting hold of the egg?'

In the background I could hear someone telling Fleet they were going to be late for class. 'Sorry, Oscar, I've got to go,' he said. 'You were right to tell me. I'll see you Wednesday, OK?'

'Fleet—' I cried.

But he'd gone.

That night I dreamed Windigo was creeping around our house in the dark whistling his dragon-charming tune. *Are you scared of magic?* he hissed in my dream.

Then he opened his mouth wide like a dragon, breathing out flames, and I shot awake, my heart pounding with fear.

Chapter Seven

BIRDIE

When Wednesday finally came round again, I was surprised to wake up to grey clouds.

'The rains are coming,' said Mum. 'When Fleet gets here I'll have to dash into Lonelyheart and stock up with shopping before the storm sets in.'

For the first time since he'd started working for my mum, Ferris Fleet was late.

I kept scrambling up and down the ladder to my tree house, expecting to catch sight of Wonderwheels zooming up the mountain, but when Fleet's wheelchair finally appeared it was from the totally opposite direction.

I slid down the ladder and raced to meet him. 'You came a different way,' I said breathlessly.

Fleet's hair was stiff with dust. He looked unusually frazzled. 'I had to make sure I wasn't followed,' he explained.

I felt a twang of fear. He meant followed by Windigo.

'I'll just tell Mum you're here,' I told him. 'She's worried about getting supplies in before it rains.'

I waited till we saw Mum's car go bumping down the track, then I said, 'Are you sure nobody followed you?'

'Not unless he's got a magic wheelchair that goes through solid rock.' Fleet was still shaking the dust out of his hair. 'Bit messy but confusing for the enemy!'

I'd forgotten Wonderwheels did stunts like that.

'Oscar, I need to ask you something.' Fleet sounded urgent. 'We're ninety-nine per cent sure it won't hatch, but we don't want Windigo to get his greedy hands on it.' Fleet reached into his bag and took out a bundle wrapped in an old flannel shirt. Slowly, carefully, he unwrapped it.

When I saw what was inside I almost stopped breathing. 'Is that—?'

I whispered.

'Yes. It's a fire dragon's egg.' Fleet was whispering too.

It was the colour that startled me most. You'd expect a dragon's egg to be big, and it was – it was bigger than my head! I just hadn't expected it to be so beautiful. I hadn't expected it to be deep berry-red with golden swirls and tiny bright speckles like stardust.

'It's the most magical thing I've ever seen in my life,' I breathed.

Fleet managed a tired smile. 'Oscar, this is a huge favour we're asking. We need you to look after the egg for a few days.'

'*Me?*' I squeaked.

'Our exams start tomorrow. We'll be in the exam hall all day, every day, until they're over. Yesterday was my turn to mind the egg. I kept popping back to my room to check it was OK, but last night when I put my key in the lock, I thought I smelled—'

'Dragon smoke,' I whispered.

'I'm always telling the others about your family. They know your mum used to be with the CPP and they said they trust you to look after it for us.'

For a minute I couldn't speak.

'I'll protect it with my life,' I said fiercely.

'Think of a hiding place,' Fleet said. 'Somewhere Windigo would never think of looking.'

I started to grin. I knew the perfect place. 'Follow me.'

Ruby and I led Fleet down the garden to meet the Bettys. The hens fluttered and fussed, wondering what was going on.

'Birdies! Birdies!' Ruby shouted.

Fleet laughed out loud. 'Oscar, you're a genius! Windigo would never dream of looking there.'

I lifted the roof of the henhouse, carefully slipping the dragon's egg under the clean straw.

All three Bettys instantly rushed in to see what I was doing. 'This is possibly the last-ever

dragon's egg on World Nine,' I told them. 'Take care of it, OK?'

Fleet stayed until Mum got back from town, then he had to leave. 'I'm sorry to let you down like this, but exams start tomorrow,' he told her.

'You shouldn't leave things till the last

minute,' she scolded. I knew Mum wasn't really cross though, because she wrapped up a huge slab of home-made cake for Fleet to share with his friends.

When I went out to wave Fleet off, I saw storm clouds piling up in the distance.

'We'll come as soon as we can,' Fleet said in a low voice. Then he zoomed off down the track. I watched until Wonderwheels was a shining multicoloured dot, then I went indoors.

I found Mum putting away the shopping.

'I've been thinking,' I said. 'It's time I did more of the work around here.'

Mum was so shocked she almost dropped a jar of honey. 'What kind of work?'

'I thought I'd start with the hens,' I said. 'From now on I'll feed the Bettys and collect their eggs.'

Mum gave me a disbelieving look.

'And clean them out?'

'And clean them out,' I gulped. Suddenly I was leading a double life: hiding a wizard's staff among the umbrellas, and now sneaking a dragon's egg into the henhouse. I wasn't sure how long I could keep it up.

★

In the end it was another three days before the rains started. They arrived in the night, thundering down on our roof and sending rivers of water gurgling into the drains.

Early next morning Mum came to see if my ceiling had sprung a leak. She'd been up half the night putting buckets and basins around the house to catch the drips.

'I'll check the Betties,' I said, yawning.

I dragged on Mum's wellies and went splashing across the garden.

The hens seemed unusually restless, fluttering and clucking as if they were trying to tell me something.

I lifted the roof of the henhouse and felt around under the straw until I found the smooth curved shape of the

egg. 'It's hot!' I cried, startled.

Next minute there was a loud *CRR-ACKK!*

The exact thing Fleet said would never happen was actually happening. The dragon's egg was hatching!

I stood hypnotized as something invisible chip-chipped away at the inside of the egg. Now that it had got started, the baby dragon seemed determined to batter its way out. The egg was practically dancing up and

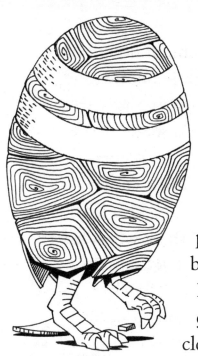

down in the straw.
CRICK!

A piece of shimmery red shell suddenly fell off. I gasped as a scaly green elbow poked out. More bits of shell flew off. I thought I saw a glittering yellow claw, but the Bettys were as excited as I was and kept blocking my view.

Then suddenly there it was: an astonished little boy dragon with enormous yellow eyes and bright green fuzz sticking up all over.

The Bettys started fussing over their strange new chick,

85

but the baby dragon dodged
them on his
wobbly new legs.
He seemed to be
looking for someone.

'Hello, dragon,' I said
softly.

He looked up at me, amazed, then he
put his head on one side and made a soft
whistling sound. I whistled back.

In a clumsy rush, he spread small
leathery wings and half
flew, half threw himself
into my arms!

'Sorry, you've got to stay
with the Bettys. They're
your mummies, not me.'
I gently put him back in
the henhouse and closed
up the roof.

I heard a distressed tooting sound, like
a teeny-tiny version of the foghorns we
heard in Terra Nova. I went splashing

back towards the house feeling like a cold-hearted monster.

Suddenly I heard scrabbling sounds and what sounded like wood splintering. Next minute something went whooshing past my ear and the baby dragon landed *splosh* at my feet.

'You can't come in,' I hissed. 'Mum mustn't see you.'

'What mustn't Mum see?' said a voice.

Mum was standing on the veranda, watching us with a most peculiar expression on her face.

Ruby had followed her out. She caught sight of the baby dragon and shrieked with laughter. 'Funny birdie!'

'Don't you think you should bring your funny birdie in out of the rain?' Mum's expression was beyond frosty. Inside the house she planted her hands on her hips. 'Any time you feel like explaining, Oscar,' she said in her coldest Peace Police voice.

I had to tell her everything. About World Nine's endangered dragons, about seeing Windigo the dragon-chaser the day we went to the library, about Fleet and his student buddies forming a group to protect the few surviving dragons.

Partway through my story, Birdie started making such desperate foghorn noises that I had to clutch my ears. 'What's wrong with him?' I panicked.

'He's probably hungry. Try giving him some porridge. All babies like porridge.' Mum sounded so calm you'd think she fed porridge to dragons every day.

Mum made the porridge, then I held Birdie on my lap and Mum expertly

spooned the milky
gloop into his
mouth. We knew
when he'd had
enough because
he immediately

fell over with all his feet in the air and
started snoring.

'Did Fleet say
how often he needs
feeding?' Mum
asked.

I shook my
head. 'Last
time Fleet saw
Birdie he was just an egg.'

'Try every two hours to start with,'
Mum suggested. She lifted the baby
dragon off my lap, gently tucking him
into Ruby's dolls' pram with her teddies
and dollies. 'How cute is he?' she said,
smiling.

Mum's reaction to the dragon's arrival

was making me seriously confused.
'Aren't you really angry?' I asked
nervously.

'You can't be angry at a baby,' Mum
said. 'I'm not upset with you either, so
stop looking so worried.'

'But you hate magic!'

She laughed. 'I know. But if what Fleet
says about dragon-chasers is true, it isn't
us that are in danger from the dragons.
It's the dragons that are in danger.' Mum
suddenly took my face in her hands.
'I'm used to working for the good guys,
remember?' she explained, smiling. 'It still
makes me *really* annoyed when the bad
guys think they can win!'

'Mum, look at Ruby,' I whispered.
'I think she got up too early.'

While we were talking my little sister
had curled up on the rug beside her
dolls' pram and fallen fast asleep.

Outside, the rain fell. Mum and I
chatted quietly while she knitted. Our
house had never felt so peaceful.

Then the phone rang. 'Who's this?'
Mum asked the caller suspiciously.
'I'm afraid I don't know anyone called
Raymond.' Her expression changed.
'Oh, I'm so sorry! You're Miss Coralie's
nephew. She's
had a bad fall?
No, no problem
at all. I'll wait
with her until
you come back
with the doctor.
I'll be with you
just as soon as
I can.'

Chapter Eight

MR BIFFIN'S WALKING STICK

'Don't go!' I begged Mum. 'It's a trick.'

Mum shook her head. 'It sounds like Miss Coralie's had a nasty fall. She shouldn't be left alone.'

Fleet was right. Dragon-chasers are patient and cunning; they watch and wait for as long as it takes; then they pounce, luring dragons from their eggs and mothers from their children. They do it by pretending to be something they're not: another dragon, someone's teenage nephew.

'You don't seriously believe that was Raymond who called you just now? You heard what Miss Coralie said.

Raymond's not the caring type. Anyway, why didn't he just ask the doctor to come out?'

'He says the doctor's got some problem with his car.' Mum was already pulling on her wellies. 'Oscar, I know it might be a trick, but I need to see Miss Coralie for myself.'

I could have begged her to stay. I could have said: 'Mum, don't go. I'm scared. The dragon-chaser isn't just a normal hunter, he's something much worse. He's some kind of evil wizard.' I didn't say any of those things. I'd spent months persuading Mum to tolerate wizards. It didn't seem right to play the wizard card now.

'Bolt the door as soon as I leave,' Mum told me. 'I'll just be five minutes. Ruby's asleep, so I'm trusting you to keep an eye on her. Don't let anyone in until I get back.'

Pulling her raincoat over her head,

she ran into the downpour. I quickly locked and bolted the door behind her even though I knew that wouldn't stop Windigo.

Birdie had woken from his nap and was happily chewing one of Ruby's teddies. I set him on the rug, where he immediately did an enormous poo. I wearily got a bucket of water and a cloth to clean it up.

When I came back Birdie was playing with a knitted throw Mum had left draped over her chair, batting its tassels with a fuzzy green paw.

I was still
scrubbing away
at the rug when
I heard a soft,
low whistle.

Instantly the
door key flew
out of the lock,
smacking me
on the head.
Next minute all
three bolts drew
back at once,
the door burst

open and Windigo stood there with rain
streaming off his beautiful dragon-skin
coat.

'Hello, Oscar,' he said. 'Long time no
see!'

He spotted Birdie peeping out from
behind the tassels and gave a shout of
laughter. 'Better and better! The little
worm actually hatched!' He crossed the

room in three strides. 'Come here, you runty lizard,' he growled.

I quickly put myself between Windigo and the dragon. 'He's just a baby. You killed his mum – isn't that enough?' I hoped he couldn't see my knees shaking.

'Out of my way, brat,' said Windigo.

I didn't move. 'What's the point of taking him? They won't let you smuggle a live dragon out of World Nine.'

'Who won't let me?' snorted Windigo.

'McCool, for one. He hates what creeps like you are doing to his world.'

The hunter picked me up with one arm and dumped me out of his way. 'McCool isn't the only fool with a starship,' he sneered.

All the shouting had woken my little sister. She sat up, bewildered. 'Mama?'

'Besides, I'll make ten times

the money for a live one! Come on, you ugly freak,' Windigo said to the dragon.

'Stop talking to Birdie like that,' I said.

'I don't need to talk, Oscar,' said Windigo. 'Don't you know that by now?' And he pursed his lips and started to whistle his eerie little dragon tune.

Birdie had been warily watching him from under Mum's chair. *Now he'll go to Windigo*, I thought miserably. *He won't be able to help it.*

But when he heard Windigo doing his cunning imitation of a dragon's song, Birdie just looked puzzled. He put his head on one side, anxously sniffed the air, then quickly backed under the chair, making scared whistling sounds down his nose like a puppy.

He knows, I thought. *He knows Windigo killed his mum.*

'Right, you little maggot, come here. I've wasted enough time on you.' Windigo lunged at the dragon.

'Don't hurt him!' I begged. 'I'll – I'll help you, OK?'

Windigo laughed in my face. 'You'll help me? Seems like you're the one who needs the help, Oscar.'

'Birdie trusts me,' I said. 'Plus it's time for his next meal. Mum said I had to feed him every two hours. Once his tummy's full he'll drop off to sleep. It'll be easier for you to take him then.'

The dragon-chaser paced up and down our kitchen while I warmed up the porridge and fed Birdie.

I kept my eyes firmly on the spoon, hoping Windigo wouldn't guess what I was planning. Like last time, when the baby dragon was full, he fell over and started snoring.

Immediately Windigo was looming over me. 'Now hand it over!'

'Not yet!' I said hastily. 'I mean, you're the dragon expert, but it can't be good for a baby fire dragon to get wet. It's chucking it down outside. I'll get Mum's umbrella.'

'All right, but get a move on,' he snarled.

I hurried out to the hall, still holding the sleeping Birdie. It was just a few steps to the umbrella stand, but it felt like a million miles. *Don't let him read my thoughts,* I prayed.

'Here it is!' I said breathlessly, running back in.

Windigo expression changed to one of extreme surprise. 'That's not an umbrella! That's a—'

'STOP WINDIGO NOW!' I screamed at Mr Biffin's staff. 'I DON'T CARE WHAT YOU DO, BUT STOP HIM HURTING BIRDIE!'

I was just a scared kid with no magical training whatsoever. I didn't know even one magic word. I just shouted out what was in my heart.

A huge purple flash came out of the staff, blowing me halfway across the room.

Somehow I hung onto Birdie. I picked myself up in a daze. Incredibly the baby dragon had slept through the whole thing.

There was no sign of Windigo – just a big hole in the floor where he'd been

standing. I peered
cautiously into
the hole.

'Gone,'
said Ruby
cheerfully.
She
pointed
under
Mum's
chair.

''Nother birdie.'

The tassels fluttered on Mum's throw
and a sky-blue chicken trotted out. I
looked at the chicken, then I looked at
the staff and my knees suddenly went
weak.

I heard voices outside and Mum came
rushing in, quickly followed by Fleet and
five or six anxious-looking students who
I took to be his friends.

'Is everyone OK?' asked Mum
breathlessly. 'Did Windigo get in here?

And what in the world happened to my floor!'

Fleet saw the chicken and started to laugh. 'Is that him?'

'Forget about Windigo,' I told him proudly. 'Meet Birdie the dragon!'

Chapter Nine

MERLIN MCCOOL SWINGS BY

I'd saved a cute baby dragon, possibly
the last one to be born on World Nine.
Unfortunately I'd had to break Mum's
rules to do it. I had used forbidden
magic, not to mention blowing a serious
hole in the floor.

'I think Oscar's got some more
explaining to do,' Mum said in her Peace
Police voice.

Her lips were twitching as if she
wanted to laugh, but she was tapping
her foot, which if you knew my mum is
a really bad sign. I looked helplessly at
Fleet. I didn't have a choice. I had to give
Mum the alarming news that nice old

Mr Biffin was most probably a wizard.

'We're living in a wizard's house and you *knew*!' Mum burst out as soon as I stopped explaining. 'How long were you planning to keep *that* little secret, Oscar!'

'I was scared you'd make us go back to Terra Nova,' I said miserably. 'I'm really sorry, Mum. I didn't mean to turn Windigo into a chicken. I just couldn't let him hurt Birdie.'

To my amazement, Mum burst out laughing. 'I'd have turned that creep into chicken pieces, given half a chance! Will he have to be a bright blue chicken for ever, do you know?' she asked Fleet with interest.

'If you want my advice, you'll keep him like that at least till he gets back to his home planet,' said a familiar voice.

A rain-soaked Merlin McCool was standing in the doorway.

I think Mum was still in shock from all the excitement, because she didn't seem surprised at all. She just accepted McCool turning up, like she'd accepted a baby dragon and an enchanted chicken.

'We can't just let this cosmic lowlife go,' she objected. 'What if he comes back looking for more dragons' eggs?'

McCool gave his lopsided grin. 'Would you go back somewhere where they'd turned you into a sky-blue chicken?'

Mum started to giggle. 'Maybe not.'

McCool looked around our big homely sitting room, where Fleet and his student buddies were making themselves comfortable. 'Hi, Fleet,' he said casually.

'Do you two know each other?' Now

Mum *was* surprised.

'Actually, we're cousins,' Fleet told her, grinning.

The first time I saw McCool I had known he looked familiar. Now they were in the same room I could see that Fleet and McCool had almost exactly the same smile.

'So, is this a private party or can anyone join in?' McCool asked my mum.

'If you want a party, Mr McCool, you'd better lend me a hand in the kitchen,' Mum told him crisply.

They went off to throw some party food together.

Fleet's friends sat around cooing over the baby dragon. It was actually really embarrassing. Birdie wouldn't let anyone touch him but me! One of the girls tried to pet him and he made such ear-splitting foghorn noises that I had to pick him up and give him a cuddle.

'You're the first person he saw when he

hatched,' Fleet explained. 'He trusts you to take care of him. When he's older we'll take him back to Firebreath Valley to live with the other dragons. Until then he might have to live with you, if that's OK with your mum?'

I sighed. 'After what just happened I'm not sure Mum will even let us stay on World Nine.'

'Your mum looks perfectly happy here just at this moment,' Fleet said mischievously. He nodded in the direction of the kitchen.

I heard McCool say, 'I brought you some seeds for your garden. Moonflowers, my favourite kind.'

I felt a smile start way down in my belly. 'Do wizards run in families?' I asked casually.

'Usually. Why do you want to know?'

'I just wondered if your cousin was one.'

'What makes you think he might be?'

Fleet said with a grin.

'Well, for one thing, McCool's starship is rusted to bits, but it flies like a bird.'

'Of course, you have to plant them by moonlight,' McCool murmured to my mum.

Mum pretended to be concentrating on making snacks, but I could tell she was smiling.

I started to laugh. It had just hit me that Mum might end up marrying a wizard after all!

HOW TO SAVE A
DRAGON

ABOUT THE AUTHOR AND ILLUSTRATOR

Annie Dalton lives in a cottage in Norfolk with a dog called Riley and three cats called Dizzee, Millie and Bo. In winter when the trees are bare she can see a ruined castle from the bottom of her garden. When she's not writing, she's reading, and when she's not reading or writing she is walking her dog and thinking about writing or reading! Annie has three children and two granddaughters – who both passionately believe in magic.

Illustrator, **Carl Pearce** lives in a little house in the mountains of north Wales. He enjoys watching films, reading books and taking long walks along the many beaches where he lives. Growing up, Carl could not decide whether to be a policeman, fireman or a GHOSTBUSTER. Instead he graduated from the North Wales School of Art and Design as an Illustrator.

Keep reading for a sneak peek at

**Ferris Fleet the Wheelchair Wizard
by Annie Dalton**

to find out what happened when Oscar
first moved to World Nine . . .

Chapter 1
THE SMALLEST GREENEST WORLD

The first time my mum left me, to go on a
secret mission for the Cosmic Peace Police (CPP),
I was only six months old. She swears she could
hear my screams all the way to the star-port.

When I was older, Mum explained why her
work took her away so much.

"I'd love to stay home, Oscar," she would sigh,
packing her overnight bag. "But I have to show
these people how to get along, instead of starting
wars."

I was proud my mum had such an important
job. As time went by, I got used to her zipping off
to a different planet every few weeks. The same
way I got used to her late night phone calls from
weird star systems no-one had ever heard of.

I got used to it. But I never liked it.

CPP baby-sitters all look the same, with their
sharp suits and blank faces. It's useless cracking a
joke. They don't know how to smile. Anyway, they
never hear a thing you tell them. Too busy talking
into their phones. As for their cooking! You can get
tired of take-away pizza, you know.

I never told Mum how I felt. She had enough
to cope with, being a cosmic troubleshooter and
bringing up a kid.

But she must have guessed, because after my
baby sister Ruby was born, Mum said she was

tired of whizzing through space, fixing people's troubles. "I keep dreaming that I live in this quiet, green little world," she said. "In my dream, all I do is grow vegetables and spend time with my beautiful children."

So she handed in her notice and went searching for the smallest, greenest world she could find.

One night, the phone rang beside my bed. "Can't talk long, Oscar," Mum yelled, through the bleeps and crackles of deepest space. "I've found this incredibly cheap house on World Nine, between the mountains and the bay. It's my dream come true."

"Grab it, quick!" I bellowed back. "Hurray!" I whispered to my little sister. "No more CPP babysitters. Ever."

I fell in love with our new home the minute we arrived. World Nine is warm and wild and there are hardly any cars, and on summer nights the air smells as sweet and spicy as pumpkin pie.

A few days after we moved in a neighbour dropped by. "My name's Miss Coralie Creek, but you can call me Coralie," she said.

I think Miss Creek was lonely. She talked more and ate faster than anyone I ever saw. And somehow, by the time she was on her fifth slice of Mum's homemade cake, she got on to wizards.

It turned out that World Nine is full of them. In fact our nearest town, Lonelyheart, has its own

116

wizards' university!

Mum didn't know whether to laugh or to cry. "You mean I've brought my children to the other end of the universe, so some cranky old wizard can turn them into frog spawn?" she wailed.

"Most wizards in Lonelyheart are harmless," Miss Creek explained. Then she lowered her voice. "The only one to watch out for is Marshbone. He's the most cold-hearted creature that ever drew breath."

She glanced nervously at the darkening sky and said she had better hurry home. Then she jumped on her bike and rode off so fast, I'm surprised her pedals didn't catch fire.

I looked up at the mountain. For the first time I noticed a strange tower hidden in the clouds. Purple lightning flickered around it.

"That's what scared Miss Creek," I thought.

When I told Mum what I suspected, she sighed and ruffled my hair. "Never mind Oscar. Our new life together is worth a wizard or two!"

But that night she locked all the doors and the windows. The next day I noticed she kept tight hold of me and Ruby when we went into town.

I'd never lived on a magic world before. I couldn't tell who were the wizards and who were just ordinary World Niners. I was extra polite to everyone, just in case.

Weeks passed and nothing happened. Unless

you count Mum getting started on her vegetable patch.

Then early one morning, a CPP starship landed outside the house. Two worried-looking men in suits got out. One of them was Mum's old boss.

"I can't believe these people! Bothering me in the middle of breakfast," Mum grumbled. But she hurried out to meet them with my sister in her arms.

A minute later she was back. "Oscar, would you bring us some iced tea?" She seemed worried and dashed straight back out.

I couldn't hear what the men were saying, but it seemed like they were trying to convince Mum of something.

She wasn't agreeing, whatever it was.

When I brought the tea out, my mother said sharply, "Our guests are starving, Oscar. Will you bring some cake, too?"

After I took out the cake tin, things went quiet, until Mum yelled for me to take Ruby for her nap.

I tried to hear what the men were saying, as I tucked my sister into her crib, but their voices were too low. It had to be something serious, to bring the head of the Cosmic Peace Police to our lonely little corner of the galaxy.

At last, the starship took off in a burst of co-loured lights. I found Mum pulling up thistles.

"Are you going away again?" I asked her.

"You know I've given up work," she replied. "My old boss just has a little problem he doesn't know how to deal with."

"Not true," I said. "Someone's starting a big war and the CPP want you to help stop it."

Mum pricked herself. "I told them to find someone else," she mumbled, sucking her bleeding finger.

"But everyone knows you're the best, Mum. If you don't go, who will?"

"I don't know. But I can't leave my babies, with some wicked wizard living at the bottom of my garden. And I hated those CPP baby-sitters as much as you did."

I knew Mum felt bad about letting her boss down. I didn't want her to go. But if she stayed home, there might be a war in space.

"What if I found a sitter," I said. "A good one. Would you go then?"

"No! Yes… I don't know…" wailed Mum. "It's impossible. The starship has to leave tomorrow night."

"That's heaps of time," I said. "We'll put up a notice at that university Miss Creek told us about."

Mum's eyebrows shot up. "The wizard university? That's like inviting the big bad wolf to sit for the three little pigs!"

Also available
from Tamarind books . . .

Spike and Ali Enson
by Malaika Rose Stanley
Illustrated by Sarah Horne

Bonnie baby or alien invader?

Everyone loves Spike's baby brother, Ali.
He's so cute even the school bullies want to
baby-sit him. But Spike isn't so sure. Ali's poos
are bright green and his soft, brown skin looks
a little scaly. Yes, there's definitely something
strange about Ali! And when Spike discovers a
way to learn the truth, he begins to realize just
how different his family really is...

ISBN 978 1 848 53023 2

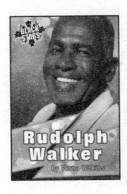

To see the rest of our list, please visit our website:

www.tamarindbooks.co.uk